THE MISSING CUPCAKE MYSTERY

Written by Tony and Lauren Dungy
with Nathan Whitaker

illustrated by
Vanessa Brantley Newton

Ready-to-Read

Simon Spotlight
New York   London   Toronto   Sydney   New Delhi

To our children: Tiara, Jamie, Eric, Jordan, Jade, Justin, Jason, and Jalen — T. D. and L. D.

"Truthful words stand the test of time, but lies are soon exposed."
— Proverbs 12:19 (NLT)

SIMON SPOTLIGHT
An imprint of Simon & Schuster Children's Publishing Division
1230 Avenue of the Americas, New York, New York 10020
Text copyright © 2013 by Tony Dungy and Lauren Dungy
Illustrations copyright © 2013 by Vanessa Brantley Newton
Published in association with the literary agency of Legacy, LLC, Winter Park, FL 32789
All rights reserved, including the right of reproduction in whole or in part in any form.
SIMON SPOTLIGHT, READY-TO-READ, and colophon are registered trademarks of
Simon & Schuster, Inc.
For information about special discounts for bulk purchases, please contact Simon & Schuster
Special Sales at 1-866-506-1949 or business@simonandschuster.com.
Manufactured in the United States of America 0915 LAK
10 9 8 7 6 5 4
Library of Congress Cataloging-in-Publication Data
Dungy, Tony.
The missing cupcake mystery / by Tony and Lauren Dungy ;
illustrated by Vanessa Brantley Newton. — 1st ed.
p. cm.
Summary: Justin, Jordan, and Jade's mother agrees to buy cupcakes if the trio will wait
until after dinner to eat them, but one cupcake goes missing and until the mystery is solved,
no one will get dessert.
[1. Family life—Fiction. 2. Cupcakes—Fiction. 3. Honesty—Fiction.] I. Dungy, Lauren.
II. Newton, Vanessa, ill. III. Title.
PZ7.D9187Mis 2012
[E]—dc23
2012024152
ISBN 978-1-4424-5463-7 (pbk)
ISBN 978-1-4424-5464-4 (hc)
ISBN 978-1-4424-5465-1 (eBook)

THE GROCERY STORE

It was grocery day!
Mom and the kids were at the store
filling their cart
with lots of yummy food.

Justin spotted boxes of cupcakes
with rainbow sprinkles. Mmm!
Jordan and Jade saw them too.
"Mom, can we get cupcakes?"
asked Jordan.
"Please, Mom?" asked Jade.
Justin said, "We've got lots of fruit.
But cupcakes would be good too."

Mom looked at the three smiling faces.
"Okay, but we all have to agree
to save them until after dinner."
Everyone agreed.
They would have the cupcakes
for dessert that evening.

HOME IN THE KITCHEN

The kids helped Mom put away
the groceries.
Jordan unpacked the cupcakes.
"Can we have one now?" he asked.

"Yes, Mom, please?" asked Jade.
"Just one?" asked Justin.
"Please, please, please," they all
chanted.

Mom reminded them that
the cupcakes were for dessert.
Everyone nodded.

Mom put the box of cupcakes in the refrigerator. Then she said, "Now go wash your hands. It's almost time for dinner."

AT THE DINNER TABLE

"What would you like on your hamburgers?" asked Dad. Jordan wanted cheese. Jade wanted ketchup.

Justin just wanted a plain
hamburger—
and some corn on the cob, potato
salad, and baked beans, too!

The whole family was enjoying Dad's hamburgers. Even Ruby! They were delicious!
"How was everyone's day at school?" asked Dad.

"We played football," said Justin.
"We played volleyball," said Jade.

"We had a math test," said Jordan,
"and it was really hard.
But I did great!"

"I'm glad everyone had a good day," said Dad.

"Me too," said Mom. "Is everybody finished eating?"

Everyone said yes, and then helped Mom and Dad clear the table.

"Time for cupcakes!" said Jordan.
"Yay!" said Justin.
"Finally!" shouted Jade.
Mom went to the refrigerator to
get the cupcakes.

She came back with a puzzled look.
"One of the cupcakes is missing,"
she said.
"Did someone eat one?" asked Dad.

"It wasn't me," said Jordan.
"Or me!" said Justin.
"It sure wasn't me," said Jade.

"Then where did it go?" asked
Justin.

The kids all looked at each other.

"Well," said Mom, "it looks like
we have quite a mystery on our
hands."

"Yes, we do have a mystery
on our hands," said Dad.
"And we need to figure it out.
No dessert until we solve
the mystery of the missing
cupcake!"
Justin, Jordan, and Jade quickly
started searching the house
for clues.

Justin and Jordan looked
everywhere.
Jade headed down the hall to her
room, and Ruby followed.

Jade sat on her bed, feeling very sad.
Ruby sat down beside Jade's bed,
and then started sniffing all around.

Ruby scratched the rug with her paw.
There she found cupcake crumbs,
and started nibbling each little one.
Mmmm!

Jade looked at Ruby.
Ruby looked at Jade.
"It was just a tiny little fib,"
Jade whispered to Ruby.
"The cupcakes looked so
delicious!"

"I didn't want to make Mom and Dad mad at me," said Jade.
Ruby looked up at Jade.
"What do you think I should do?" Jade asked Ruby.

Ruby walked to the door and
looked back at Jade.
"Ruby, you are right," said Jade.
"I should tell them the truth."

THE TRUE STORY

Jade walked back to the kitchen.
"I need to tell you something,"
Jade said softly.
"I ate the cupcake."

"We are sad, and we are happy," replied Mom.
"We are sad that you disobeyed, but happy that you told us the truth."

"You must always tell the truth,"
said Dad.
"All the time," said Mom.
"I will," Jade promised.

"Okay, the mystery is solved!"
said Dad.
"We can have dessert now, but,
Jade, you already had your cupcake.

"Okay," Jade agreed.
"That's fair."
Mom and Dad hugged her.
"We are proud of you!"

And Ruby was proud of Jade too!